The Adventures of Bertram Be

Published by Mithra Publishing in 2016
www.mithrapublishing.com

The Adventures of Bertram Bear

Best Wishes

Gregory Evans

About The Author

Gregory Gower was born in 1935 – so growing up and schooling were mixed with a world in turmoil. Most persons have the luxury of not experiencing bombs being dropped on them. He was four years of age when the war started and ten when it ended. Many days and nights were spent in an air raid shelter having to cope with listening to a gun emplacement nearby firing at enemy aircraft who were dropping their deadly cargo over Kent.

A noise so loud you would have thought your ears would have burst. His house had a direct hit and he was still in bed fast asleep when the curtains and the foot of his bed caught alight and he was rescued by a A.R.P. Warden! Many houses were destroyed and damaged later when the first of the many doodlebugs dived into the road.

He managed to gain his 11 plus at the age of 13. He went to Westwood Secondary Modern School then onto Dartford Grammar School. First job was training as a Compositor in Posners, Walters and Harrisons, Shoe Lane, Fleet Street. Second job was with Jones and Darke Rubber Plantation Office in Fenchurch Street.

He joined the Royal Air Force in 1953. Was sent abroad and served in Aden where experienced active service. Five months later he was posted to a Fighter Station/Staging Post at Sharjah where he served out the remainder of his service. On leaving the Royal Air Force, he became a Civil Servant and worked in the Passport Office and then transferred to 13 Downing Street in the United Nations Department.

Became seriously ill in 1962 and ended up in the Neurological Ward at Brooke Hospital – not expected to live! After many operations and unusual x-ray tests, the diagnosis after two years was that he had a strain of Multiple Sclerosis.

In 1976 met Brenda and after a short engagement, married her in 1977. They have one Ginger cat called Josie who brings in leaves and feathers, but no mice – yet!

He is an acting/singing member of Eastbourne Gilbert and Sullivan Society. He is editor for NODA National Operatic & Dramatic Association News Magazine for South East England. A columnist for a on-line Newspaper – thesussexnewspaper.com. Read the GG Column. A collection Secretary for N.C.H. Action for Children Charity in Eastbourne and is a member of Eastbourne Central Methodist Church Choir.

Other books by the same author:

Picture Poetry Painting Book
Derbyshire Reflections & Others) Poetry, Prose
With Mixed Feelings   ) & Goodness Knows
Food For Thought   Poetry, Prose & Recipes

A Touch of Heaven & Other Short Stories
I Remember it Well & other Short Stories
Christmas is Coming Short Stories & Sketches
Mistaken Identity
A Joyride to Murder & The Steal

In the Pipeline
A Sequel to Murder & TIME
The Christmas Tree Story   Illustrations by Amanda Breach
The Treasure   Illustrations by Amanda Breach
It Can Happen in a Week
Rhyme & Reason Poetry & Prose - some new, some old

Future projects
Hidden Agenda
Stranglehold
Enigma
Inspector Graves Investigates

Living With Hope - Autobiography

Chapter 1

Bertram Bear was Brian's best friend and everywhere Brian went, Bertram would be clutched close to his chest. He was really everything to Brian, much more than the figure of eight racing track with its red and blue cars and much more than the spanking new computer that he had been given for his ninth birthday. If Bertram had been a human he would have been a daredevil type. The expression in his eyes had that bravado look.

Brian's last sighting of Bertram would be when he closed his eyes to go to sleep as he cradled him in his arms.

No sooner had Brian fallen asleep, Bertram would suddenly wake up and try to remove himself from Brian's grip. Once free he decided he would investigate the room. It appeared to be very large and Bertram thought that when Brian breathed it was like being on a boat and that it was great fun riding up and down on Brian's chest.

Each night he would venture further and further away from the bed and this particular night he found himself in a big open space with lots of steps going down, but he being an adventurer decided to ride the banister. He did that five times and on the last climb up he was very weary.

Brian's bedroom door was always left open, just in case he had difficulty sleeping or some other nightmarish problem and should he wake up while he was on one of his adventures, Bertram would turn back into a cuddly bear. On nights when Bertram didn't get back on time Brian would scream out that he had lost his bear. His mother would rush in and say to Brian, 'He's fallen off the bed. You must have knocked him off.' She would pick the bear up and say to Brian, 'Here he is my darling. Now be a good boy and go to sleep.'

Bertram decided he was going to risk going off on another adventure and he found the figure eight car track and although he was bigger than the car he sat on the red one and whizzed round the track but kept falling off at the bends and bridge.

He thought he was in paradise; so many things to do. In the kitchen he found a swimming pool. It looked rather dirty and there were things laying beneath the surface. He didn't like the look of and gave it a wide berth.

He climbed the steps back up to bed because he could see the early morning sun filtering through the dawn clouds. It was time to resume his time with Brian.

He walked into the bedroom and there was a cat sniffing everywhere he could get its nose into. 'Hello' said bear, 'what is your name?'

'I'm Thomas the cat' said Thomas 'and who are you?'

'I'm Bertram Bear and I am Brian's best friend'.

'Any friend of Brian is my friend' said Thomas.

Bertram said 'Can you help me please? I need to get back on Brian's bed and I'm too weary to climb up those sheets.'

Thomas said 'Climb on my back and hold on very tight' and Thomas sprang effortlessly onto Brian's bed.

They landed on Brian's feet who woke up and watched as Thomas with Bertram still on his back walked up the bed but he was still trying to wake up properly and by that time Thomas had laid down in front of Brian and somehow

Bertram was once more in Brian's hands. Thomas was purring very loudly and he had a smile on his face.

Chapter 2

Bertram began to get bolder as each night approached and passed and when Brian fell asleep on this particular night, he abseiled down the sheets on the bed and then took a long run and slid on the shiny surface into this big space and climbed a post and slid down the banister. He had on occasions yelled at the top of his voice, 'Hip-hip-hooray!' which would wake the human mother and father who would rush out together to the large space and say to each other 'I thought I heard a noise' and on some occasions Bertram would be seen and picked up and taken back to Brian's room. So when he slid down the banister the second time he kept quiet.

Bertram met Thomas in the kitchen who was just yawning, stretching backwards on his haunches and then forward on his chest then giving himself a shake all over. 'Hello!' said Bertram 'How are you tonight?' There was always the same answer 'tired!' said Thomas.

Bertram asked Thomas whether it was possible to go outside. 'Anything is possible my friend,' said Thomas.

'Can we then?' said Bertram.'

'Yes!' said Thomas. 'Just climb on my back and hold onto my collar. You see this magnet, that's my front door key for getting in and out of this house. One of the members of my staff trained me that if I place my paws in a certain place the magnet will open my door, so hold on tight. It will only be a slight hoppy-jump and we'll be out.' And they were.

'What do you want to do?'

'Climb a fence,' said Bertram.

'Done that.' said Thomas.

'Well I would like to do that all the same.' So Thomas and Bertram climbed the fence.

'What do you want to do now?' said Thomas.

'Sing!' said Bertram.

'Done that!' said Thomas.

'We could sing a duet.' said Bertram.

'Done that!' said Thomas.

'The trouble with singing people throw things at you like old boots and shoes and once someone threw an alarm clock at me. It was ringing as it passed me and landed in the next garden and the next morning the man had to climb over his neighbour's fence to get it back. It was so funny to watch and I laughed so much I nearly fell off the fence. It wouldn't be too bad if they threw food at you but they don't.'

'Does that horrible dog still live here?' said Bertram.

'Yes!' said Thomas. 'But how do you know about him?'

'Mitch told me about him the other evening when I decided to stay in. Mitch is the other bear and sits on the shelf in Brian's room. The dog got through the fence and ripped off Mitch's right arm. Brian's mother sewed it back on, but Mitch lost his confidence in doing things so he just sits there looking glum. Occasionally Brian gives him a hug which is rather kind of him and I give him a salute every night which brings a smile to his lips for a while.'

Thomas said 'I often dangle my long tail and swish it backwards and forwards which drives the dog up the wall and he tries so desperately to get hold of it and in the end he barks very loudly and I disappear quickly. He told me the other day that I was on his hit list. I'll just have to be careful. Every now and then I have to eat grass and then I could be in a lot of trouble if he creeps up behind me when I'm doing that, I won't have four legs to stand on. The problem gets worse when I get fur-balls. I just freeze and I can't move at all when that happens.'

'Perhaps I can guard you when that happens,' said Bertram.

'No! You don't want to end up like Mitch do you?' said Thomas. 'Anyway it's almost dawn. I better get you back before Brian wakes up.' And he did.

Chapter 3

One of the best things Bertram liked doing was riding on Thomas's back. They would play Cowboys and Indians, Bertram of course was the cowboy and Thomas was his horse. Thomas always watched the television with the family and his favourite was John Wayne. Let's be honest Thomas liked anything that moved; he could never understand why. He used to make a fool of himself by chasing a bit of string. It seemed to please the grown-ups and he didn't mind that so much but when Brian was in a naughty mood, he had his tail pulled and he showed Brian his teeth and make hideous noises. It always seemed to work and Brian would let go of his tail immediately and say sorry to Thomas, who would always accept an apology quite happily and would rub his flanks against Brian's legs to show he had forgiven him.

By the light of the moon bear and cat could be seen doing their rodeo tricks and one night they ventured into the garden of George the dog next door and the owners could not understand how their pet dog had been tied up by the legs with twine and hanging from the point on top of his kennel. It was a mystery to them how it always happened on some nights.

George always appeared in all of Bertram and Thomas's escapades and thoroughly enjoyed himself eventually, apart from when he was trussed up like a Turkey and they left him hanging on his kennel.

George, Thomas and Bertram became firm friends and one night George apologised for tearing up Mitch. He hadn't understood, because his owners had given him a rag doll which he always played with and understandably had a momentarily lapse of memory and a mistaken identity crisis and thought Mitch was his plaything. Mitch heard this through Bertram's interpretation as Mitch was not ready to face the world outside. Bertram reported back to George that Mitch accepted his apology and would come to see George later on. George felt good on hearing this and you could almost see a halo appear over his head.

It was always going to be a one sided thing playing Cowboys and Indians and as they were always going to be the good guys, anything else that moved around at night had to be the Indians. They excluded Charles the Hedgehog, as he was too prickly and the string always broke when they tried to tie him up. Alfred the Badger was too big and Fred the Fox was too wily and Bertram and Thomas always ended up trussed like a Turkey and it usually took them ages to undo themselves and get back into Brian's bedroom before sun up.

Chapter 4

Charlie the Hedgehog moved to the back of Thomas's house for his usual bowl of cat food and saucer of milk. Thomas always very generously allowed this to happen on occasions.

Charlie knew that the house belonged to Thomas because Thomas told him that it was his and he had staff to cater for his every whim and he asked a member of his staff to supply extra rations for his friend Charlie. Thomas always felt he was doing his bit for nature. Feeding others worse off than himself.

Some nights he wanted to be alone with his thoughts and although Bertram was great fun to be with, he needed some nights of solace. He lay under the stars and watched them twinkle.

Laying on his back he felt if he stretched out his paws he could touch them, but he never could. 'Just as well,' said Thomas 'They are too bright and liable to wake up the neighbours.'

Thomas liked to lay in the garden on balmy nights. He felt contented with life. His staff always made sure his life was good and he would doze off into a deep sleep with a distant hoot from an owl in a tree a long, long away.

When the weather turned nasty and it was wet and windy he would visit George in his kennel. He and George would have a chin-wag putting the world to rights. Sometimes George could be a bit boring by chewing his bone, making slurping noises and interrupting Thomas's flow of words.

They would be lost by his noisy eating. But some nights with George were just a magic mixture of anecdotes and other escapades that both of them had experienced. Even though they were an unlikely couple to become friends, they didn't want some nights to end and they would fall asleep together.

Some nights he wanted to be alone with his thoughts and although Bertram was great fun to be with, he needed some nights of solace. He lay under the stars and watched them twinkle.

Chapter 5

'Thomas! Thomas! Breakfast!' Thomas said a hasty goodbye to George and thanked him for a pleasant evening and scrambled over the fence through the cat flap and there on the floor was his favourite food, rabbit and chicken pieces in jelly. It was like having the main meal with dessert, jelly being another one of his favourite foods.

Thomas's only wish was he didn't like his staff being so familiar with his name in public. He liked to keep a bit of mystery about himself and Thomas was his actual secret name because you know dear reader that cats have a secret name only known to themselves. It was handed down in Egyptian times many many years ago as the ancient scriptures foretold that the cat symbol was to be exalted above all. Even the Pharoahs (they were the Kings of that country a long time ago) could not attain a higher rank than a cat.

Thomas believed in all this because he had come from a very good home and his parents, although only knowing them briefly, had been taught well.

He remembered he had lots of Brothers and Sisters, but as the Egyptians would say, only one King can rule a domain. So the Robinson family decided just to have Thomas and brought him home.

He was loved as a King should be and he was surprised when they called him Thomas, his secret name. He tried to put them off by ignoring them when they called but that was no good. They kept persisting and eventually he had to respond to his given name. He was proud and in his pride he bestowed upon the family his love and loyalty and trying not to miss the dirt box when going to the toilet.

Thomas thought about his brothers and sisters and wondered where they were and only hoped that they had all found wonderful kingdoms to rule over, as he had been fortunate to have at his paws.

He always had a strong feeling that he should search beyond the borders, to go further and see what it was like in other Kingdoms, but he managed to squash the temptations of travelling. For one thing, he was afraid that if he went away, his staff would get another king to rule in his place and he couldn't risk that. He was happy with his lot.

Chapter 6

Bertram and Mitch became very close friends and Bertram was extolling the virtues of George and trying to build up Mitch's confidence. Brian's mum always puts Bertram on the shelf while Brian was at school and lately Bertram has been able to speak to Mitch during the daylight hours. It can only mean that Brian had fallen asleep at school or that he, Bertram had been given new powers and he hoped it might be the latter. When Brian came home from school Bertram and Mitch became stuffed toys again. This time Mitch was taken downstairs to Brian's figure of eight car track and Brian tied Mitch onto one the cars and off it went.

Mitch, although glassy eyed, felt rather uneasy as he hurtled round the figure of eight track and because he was a lot smaller than Bertram, he was able to go under the bridge, his head missing the bridge underneath part by half a centimetre. Mitch tried to close his eyes, but realised he hadn't any eyelids and then he also realised that he had come alive, so that meant that Brian had fallen asleep at the controls.

Mitch tried to think of it as an adventure since his last one with the dog but he was beginning to feel dizzy and ill. The figure of eight track was laid out on a platform four feet from the ground and Mitch was wondering where he was going to land if Brian's hand slipped and he went faster.

That never happened, but something else did, for he was going round so fast the whole track vibrated and the track was coming apart and as luck would have it, the straight piece came away from the bendy bit and Mitch and the car sailed through the air, through an open window, somersaulting as he went but luckily landed on all four wheels on the path that eventually led to the front gate. Mitch had to decide whether to duck under the gate or hit it. If he hit the gate he might fall to pieces again or if he ducked he might get run over by the passing cars.

George was coming back from giving his master a walk round the block and he saw the whole incident happening before his eyes. He needed to get away and he tugged so hard that his master dropped the lead. George ran to the gate, pushed it open and laid down with his back to the on-coming car with Mitch yelling frantically and flapping his arms about. George's brave action saved the day as Mitch hurtled into the softness of George.

George got up and somehow turned the car round and pushed Mitch still tied to the car with his nose back to the doorstep and barked three times.

Brian's mum came to the door and looked at George and George looked down at Mitch to notify the person about Mitch being tied to the car. 'Oh dear! Thank you George.' She picked up the car and as she closed the door she murmured 'I'm sure that dog smiled at me.'

George was elated. Somebody else knew his name and he saved Mitch from a certain something, although he didn't know what.

Chapter 7

George didn't have to tell anybody. It was around the neighbourhood that George the dog had saved the stuffing of a Bear from that certain something that they couldn't think of. All the toys in each dwelling were going to celebrate the good news. Bertram Bear was wreathed in smiles and so was Thomas and as night fell, Bertram, Mitch and Thomas met in the kitchen and walked out through the cat flap, across the garden and under the fence and gathered round George. Congratulations were in order for George for his prompt and brave action in saving Mitch from that certain something.

Unfortunately while all these celebrations were going on, Brian woke up and screamed very loudly. He wasn't feeling very well and was probably going to be up all night.

Immediately Bertram and Mitch had that stony glass eyed stare and just sat there looking at George.

George turned to Thomas. 'What are we going to do now?'

Thomas thought for a moment and then said 'Have you got any string?' George said. 'What ideas have you got up your hairy armpits now?' Thomas said 'If you tie Mitch onto my shoulders I'll try and sneak him back into the house. I don't know what we're going to do about Bertram. I can't carry him under the fence he's too big. I'll think about him on my way with Mitch.'

Thomas felt like he was part of the secret Service and was on a cloak and dagger mission. He tried to tip-toe across the paved area but it hurt his paws and with that extra dead weight load, it made it difficult for him to keep his balance properly. He had learnt to get on his hind legs and move like a human. It was a habit he got into from watching too many gangster movies. He couldn't do that, because he would squash Mitch when he leant backwards, so he would have to move like a cat should do.

Getting through the cat flap was going to be difficult. It would have to be commando style and crouching was in order as Thomas opened his cat flap door. He leapt low scraping his stomach on the bar that kept the contraption together. He felt sore, but squaring his shoulders and just remembering his load in time he pushed on. He should get a medal for his actions tonight he thought. He slithered up the stairs as best as one could slither and reached the landing. His heart pounded away at eighty beats to the minute and didn't know if that was correct or not for a cat under stress.

Chapter 8

Thomas darted into the dimly lit room. Brian was sitting up with something sticking out of his mouth with a man holding his wrist and looking at his watch at the same time. Thomas thought that the man wanted to get away quickly, which was why probably he was looking at his watch.

The next problem was, how was he going to release Mitch from his back? An idea popped into his head. Mitch is just a toy, I'll shake myself really quickly and as he did Mitch slid underneath him and Thomas was able to use his sharp claws to cut through the string. He picked up Mitch and placed him under the shelf unit and meowed loudly. Mother looked round but Thomas had already disappeared. Mother saw Mitch and picked him up and said to Brian 'I've found Mitch, I'll look for Bertram in a minute, but let's wait to hear what the Doctor says.'

The Doctor said 'You'll need to get some antibiotics, he has a bit of a temperature, nothing to worry about. I have some in my bag for tonight, but tomorrow get these tablets at the chemist as soon as it opens.' The Doctor wrote out the prescription and handed it to mum. 'I'm afraid your son won't sleep much tonight. He must have plenty of water.'

Thomas thought, 'Brian will be awake all night. I was listening on the landing. He's got to take tablets and have plenty of water so he will be up all night for sure. While the Doctor is writing out his chit for medicine and telling one of my staff what she has to do to make Brian better I am going to dash round to the front door and there might be a chance of getting Bertram back without any problem.'

The Doctor said goodnight to mum and dad and went out of the front door as Thomas came in with Bertram's arm in his mouth. The Doctor and Thomas passed each other on the threshold of the door.

The Doctor looked down as Thomas walked by with this thing in his mouth. Thomas walked up the stairs and dropped Bertram just inside the bedroom door and went as silently as he could out through the cat flap to report to George that everything was back to normal.

Chapter 9

Brian had at last fallen asleep and Bertram found himself sitting against the bedroom door. How he got there was a mystery, because his last recollection was of standing with George, congratulating him on his heroic action in saving Mitch from something. That seemed ages ago.

While he was sitting there wondering what action to take next a young Owl flew into the room. He said 'I'm lost! I can't seem to find my mum and dad. All the trees look the same to me. Can you help me?'

'We'll try' said Bertram 'I just have to get my friends to help. What's your name?'

'My mum and dad have named me Al. I think that's a funny name for me.'

'Why?' said Bertram. 'I'll be known as Al the Owl.' he said.

Bertram remarked 'That he thought the name had a certain poetic ring about it, almost tuneful.'

'I don't like it.' said Al, 'Poetic or not.'

Thomas and George were basking in the early morning sun and listening to the conversation between Bertram and the Owl. They both muttered, 'Here we go again, another adventure.'

'Hold on a second.' he said to Al. Bertram scaled up the overhanging sheets on Brian's bed and clambered onto the window sill and Bertram climbed down the drainpipe and Al the Owl flew down to where Thomas and George were laying.

Bertram poked Thomas. 'Come on lazy bones, get up! Work to do.' George lay very still pretending to be asleep. Thomas didn't want to move again after all his trouble last night to get Mitch and Bertram back to Brian's bedroom. It seemed like all work and no play lately and neither Thomas or George could muster the strength to wake up let alone stand up.

'Looks like we're not going to get any help today Al.'

'Oh!' Sobbed Al, 'I'll never find my mummy and daddy now.'

George got up first and said 'I hate it when kids cry, it really tugs at your heart strings, doesn't it.' George lifted his right paw and thumped his chest where he thought his heart was.

Thomas said, 'Oh well sleep can wait awhile.' He yawned and at the same time made a hideous noise.

Al said, 'You'll all have to keep your wits about you. There's a very big bird out there and that's why I flew into that open window this morning' and pointed his wing at the window. 'I think he thought I was his breakfast.'

'How big is big?' said Thomas flexing his left paw. Each needle sharp claw sparkled as it flew from the paw into the air as Thomas did an imaginary battle with an invisible foe.

'Bigger than you' said Al.

'Well perhaps not today.' said Thomas 'It's too hot for fighting.' Each claw disappeared back inside his paw.

George said, 'What's the plan then to find Al's tree?'

Bertram said 'As I see it, we will need someone who can climb trees and that is your job Thomas, and George, you will be the contact and tracker on the ground.' 'What are you going to do Bertram?' said George. 'I shall be there to give moral support and back up for plan B,' Bertram replied. 'What's plan B?' said George.

'I don't know at the moment, but I'm working on it,' said Bertram. Thomas made a giant leap and landed on the lower branches of the first tree of the many that lay before them.

Chapter 10

Something strange started to happen to Bertram which he had never felt before. He wondered whether it had something to do with the sun and wished he was wearing a sun hat. For a bear he was making good progress along the path at the bottom of the garden and was wondering if he would be able to catch up with the others when there was a shout from the house.

He turned and could not believe what he saw. It was Brian leaning out of the window. Bertram stopped in his tracks. He knew what should have happened, but it hadn't. He would have to pretend he was just a stuffed toy and that might present itself as a bit of a problem when your heart is beating nineteen to the dozen.

Bertram sat down with a thump and tried to look glassy-eyed. It was no good, perhaps Brian had not realised he was walking because it was at a distance when the shout came.

Obviously Bertram couldn't answer back as that would have given the game away. Brian shouted at the top of his voice. 'What are you doing down there?' Surely, thought Bertram he doesn't expect me to answer. Brian repeated the question. Bertram pinched himself. It hurt.

Can this be real? Bertram happened to glance towards the greenhouse and the reflection that came back to him would have knocked him off of his feet had he'd been standing. He was a little boy.

This is mad thought Bertram perhaps the sun had been too strong after all and given him sunstroke. There was another shout from the window from Brian. 'Do you know you are trespassing? This is private property!'

Bertram could hardly turn round and say he was Brian's bear. He shouted back 'Sorry!' Got up and ran as fast as he could towards the woods beyond the bottom of the garden.

What was bear going to say to the others if and when he caught up with them? Then he saw them. Al the Owl was flying while Thomas gracefully jumped from tree branch to another branch. George was tracking and looking up and saying. 'Seen anything yet?'

'No!' said Thomas 'I'll let you know if anything comes into view.'

Bertram caught up with them puffing and gasping for breath. George turned round and said 'About time where have you been? Have you come up with plan B yet. It's been a lonely trek without you.

Bertram was dumbfounded. Had he changed back to being a bear? He pinched himself again and it hurt. No, obviously not. Bertram said to George 'Do you see anything different about my appearance?'

'No!' said George 'Should there be. Maybe you look taller.'

'Hey! You two! Can we get on with what we're supposed to be doing, instead all this chat about how we are looking this morning. You look fine Bertram. Maybe a bit taller.'

Al said nothing.

Oh well thought Bertram, if they haven't noticed the difference then that's okay.

'Oh oh,' said Thomas 'We have a problem.' Swooping down towards them was this enormous bird. It whizzed passed Thomas who spun round and round on the branch by the force of his slipstream.

Thomas managed to keep his balance. George barked, Al hooted, Bertram shouted, Thomas snarled.

The bird settled on an adjacent tree branch and said his name was Peregrine and he said, 'I'm lost! I was going to ask that young owl there the way to Godstone Tower, but he mistook my intentions and flew off.' Bertram said 'What are you doing so far into the countryside?'

'My very first day at flying and I've gone too far. I was enjoying myself so much I forgot about time and being cooped up in a nest for such a long time gave me cramp in my legs, I just had to get out. Now I have lost my home bearings. Al hooted in agreement. 'I've forgotten where my mummy and daddy's tree is. Peregrine nodded all knowingly.

'We seem to have double trouble.' said Bertram.

Chapter 11

'Triple trouble.' said Al to Bertram. 'What do you mean by triple?' 'You're a boy' said Al.

Bertram stared at the Owl. 'How do you know? And why can't the others see the difference?'

Al said, 'I don't know the answer to that one.'

Peregrine said 'Can I travel with you?'

'Yes of course you can.' said Bertram.

'Thank you! I might even find your parents young Owl. My eyes are eagle sharp and I can usually spot something three hundred feet away.' Peregrine looked straight ahead then to left and then to the right and there he saw something on a branch almost the same colour as the branch and pointed with his wing.

'We have to swing to starboard.' said Peregrine 'Seven trees away.' Thomas leapt from branch to branch and tree to tree and as he got nearer and nearer there before him were two very worried looking owls. Thomas shouted 'We've found your son, Al. He's not far behind.'

Next to arrive was George, then Bertram, Al and Peregrine. Hugs between the parents and Al were very moving and mother owl wiped a tear from her face.

Father Owl spoke to Peregrine and said, 'Your father came to see me and has left instructions that should I meet up with you. I was to tell you the map references you need to know to get you back home.'

Peregrine could have hugged father Owl but didn't. Father Owl gave Peregrine the instructions he needed and after much shaking of wings and paws and hand. Peregrine flew off.

They all watched until he was just a speck in the sky and then vanished completely from their view.

Bertram, Thomas and George said goodbye to the owl family and made their way back to Brian's house.

On the way home Thomas said to Bertram 'Do you think you'll turn back into a bear before we get back to the house?'

Bertram said 'You noticed then.' 'Of course we did.' said Thomas. 'Anyone who can grow two feet taller in minutes and look so strange has got to be different.'

George said 'We didn't like to say because of Owl's problem and then Peregrine's dilemma. Now we have resolved their problems we'll have to wait and see what happens to you.'

Eventually they reached the border of where the woods end and where Brian's garden began when Bertram got that funny feeling as before and he became a bear again.

The sun was going down and they realised that they had been away for the whole day. Thomas rushed into the kitchen and ate his food, and drank all the water.

Brian's mum came into the kitchen. 'Where have you been all day? We've been calling you for ages. We thought we had lost you.' Thomas just sat and looked at his human mum and asked for more food which he eventually got.

George sloped off to his kennel and got the same treatment. They were glad to see him back but neither could tell their human parents what adventures they had experienced. Bertram sneaked passed Thomas's mum and climbed the stairs to the landing as he had heard it called one day the week before and stepped into Brian's room. Brian was awake and reading and he looked a lot better than the last time Bertram had seen him and Bertram was wondering why he was still walking because Brian was awake.

'Ah! There you are said Brian, I wondered when you were coming back.' 'You can see me walk and hear me talk?' said Bertram. 'Of course!' said Brian 'I also know you can talk to animals and birds and they talk to you.' 'Oh no! said Bertram, 'The secret's out!.

Bertram woke up with a start on the window ledge and found the wind blowing into his face and turned round and found Brian sleeping. How he got there was a mystery. He last remembered standing with George congratulating him for his heroic action in saving Mitch from that certain something. 'So it was a dream, thank goodness!' said Bertram.

Chapter 12

Charlie the Hedgehog decided to pay another visit to Thomas's house. This time it was for another reason, although a bowl of bread and milk would be nice to have. Trouble is you couldn't always get what you wished for in life.

Thomas said 'Hello Charlie! Would you like something to eat and drink?' 'I wouldn't mind a bowl of hot milk and bread, I've got a bit of a chesty cold, I need looking after for a while.' Charlie made a rasping sound which certainly sounded like a bad cold.

As it happened the human mum was around when Charlie was making these noises and Charlie received what he wished for. Thomas thought I might start using ploys like that when I want something special to eat. After Charlie had finished his meal he showed Thomas his scars where someone had tried to take his quills out.

'Who did that to you?' said Thomas.

'I don't rightly know.' said Charlie. I was near this gypsy encampment one night warming myself by their fire when I felt someone tugging at my spikes and three of them just went. They were near my tummy and it's a bit sore and has been bleeding, I just wondered if you knew something about second aid?'

'No!' said Thomas 'But its not called second, it's first aid.' Thomas asked Charlie to roll over and Thomas went to get his human mother and she followed Thomas back into the kitchen and saw the damage and said 'You poor sweetie, I'll take you to the vet.'

The human mother found a cardboard box lined it with some cloth and placed Charlie very carefully in the box and went out the front door. Thomas went out through his cat flap and went to see George and told him all about Charlie's wounds.

George said 'How cruel! But what can we do?' 'Well I suppose we could try to find this Gypsy caravan and do something. Let's have a word with Bertram, he might know what to do.'

Bertram was still sitting on the window ledge fanning himself with a feather he had found. He looked perturbed about something. Thomas shouted up to him and asked him to come down. Bertram climbed down one of the drainpipes nearest to him and was told of the dreadful injuries that Charlie had and that Thomas's human mother had taken Charlie to someone who knew first aid.

'What's that?' said Bertram. 'Something that you'll never need.' said George.

Bertram said 'Lets wait till Charlie comes back.' They all went back to their separate places.

But Charlie never came back with Thomas's human mother and Thomas was fretting walking backwards and forwards and getting on his hind legs and placing his paws on her lap.

She said to Thomas 'Don't worry my clever little boy, your hedgehog friend has to stay in hospital for a while. He'll be okay soon.'

Thomas was frantic to tell everyone the good news about Charlie and that he had to stay in hospital whatever that was but he would be back soon.

Chapter 13

When Charlie eventually came back he was bandaged up and Thomas's human mother said she would look after the hedgehog until he was better. Charlie and Thomas ate together and some nights slept together for quite a long time. Charlie had a fresh cardboard box every night, so his wounds would not get an infection and he was given tablets by Thomas's human mother every day. She took Charlie to see his first aid human and received a clean bill of health. She told Thomas who seemed overjoyed by the news and Charlie was allowed to go out into the back garden again.

Charlie decided that Thomas's back garden was a fair size and that he would not venture beyond the borders as doing so led him to danger and besides the occasional square meal from Thomas's kitchen staff was much appreciated.

Brian was still weak from his infection and his parents made sure he went to bed at an earlier time until he had recovered one hundred percent. He would sit in bed and read for a while until the sleepy dust closed his eyes and he fell asleep.

*　　　　*　　　　*　　　　*

Mitch yawned. He felt that this was a good time as any to face the world and George the dog, who he had forgiven for mistakenly thinking he was a ragdoll and so had given those injuries to him.

On the shelf where he usually sat was a ball of string and a box of drawing pins. Mitch didn't ask for any help, he was going to use his brains and be adventurous himself.

Mitch wasn't very big but he thought he might be able to work something out with these two items being placed in a certain way. He emptied the box of drawing pins on the shelf and they rolled round and round and some fell off the shelf.

The ball of string was nearly the same height as Mitch, but he had that determined look in his eyes.

He picked up a drawing pin and placing the point downwards into the shelf, he hoped that by sitting on it, it would sink into the wood, but it didn't. Mitch looked around the shelf and he saw a small pair of scissors and started bashing the drawing pin with the handle end of the scissors and slowly the drawing pin went into the wood. He unwound the string until the end touched the floor and with another drawing pin pierced the end of string and at a certain angle managed to knock this pin in and with more string he wound this round the other pin, wiped his forehead with his paw and went 'phew!' and sat down with a thump. 'That was hard work!' He pulled the string and it held and he slid down it and as he reached the floor, the ball of string landed beside him and rolled out of Brian's room across the landing and bounced down the stairs unravelling as it went, across the hallway and hit the lounge door where it stopped.

Mitch struggled down the stairs and into the kitchen and out of the cat flap and walked across where Thomas was laying under a bush, shading himself from the last of the suns rays.

Mitch said 'Hello Thomas!'

Thomas looked round in disbelief. 'Ahh! You've managed to get your nerve up and come out.'

'Yes!' said Mitch. 'Brian's gone to sleep, so I thought I would come down and see you.'

Thomas didn't want to offend Mitch by saying if Brian was awake, they wouldn't be talking to each other.

Thomas said 'Come on Mitch, let's go and meet George. They walked across the grass towards that part of the fence that had a hole in it and since that night when Bertram and Mitch were stranded in the garden, George had dug his side of the garden fence to make it easier for the bears to enter instead of having to climb over the fence.

George was laying half in and half out of his kennel and when he saw Mitch approaching he leapt out of the kennel and his tail wagged at such a pace he almost fell over.

'Oh Mitch it is so nice to see you at last, and you're looking fit and well.'

Bertram came down from the window ledge where he liked to sit and catch the wind, for he found it was lovely when it ruffled his fur and he liked to hear nature with its different sounds out in the garden. Brian had not cuddled him for ages and in a way he was pleased because after a while he felt very hot and stifled and he needed the night air to recover. Bertram said hello to Mitch and how nice it was to see him in the garden.

They sat round in a circle and discussed whether they should follow up what happened to Charlie and how could any of them do anything to avenge what agonising torture Charlie had to endure. They decided unanimously that in this instance they would not do anything. Besides, as Bertram pointed out the caravan might have moved on and it would be a long, long journey in the dark and they might not get back in time by sunrise. Somebody said any other business and the answer was 'No!'

Chapter 14

Nick the Magpie decided to visit Thomas's garden the next day. He was called Nick because he kept nicking things that weren't his property and taking them back to his nest. He was a very chirpy sort and always had a grin on his face and he had learned a trick or two from Sammy the Seagull that if you wanted a big fat worm you needed to learn how to tap dance on the grass. Sammy taught Nick this one, two, one step and if you did it quickly enough it brought out the worms who usually were holding their heads complaining they had headaches and before they could get a miracle cure they were all swallowed up.

When the human mother did the washing up she placed her ring on a porcelain finger especially made for rings as a safeguard for not losing it down the plug hole.

Unfortunately that evening Nick, being the daredevil he was, flew through the kitchen window and stole the ring. The human mother watched her ring disappear into the trees and began to cry. The human father came running in and she told him what had happened.

Thomas was witness to all of this and decided with the help of his large circle of friends that they were going to get back her ring, because he remembered her kindness shown to Charlie the Hedgehog.

A meeting was convened. Bertram wished that Peregrine and Al the Owl were real, but they had been in a dream, his dream. He had turned into a boy. But then again some secrets had to be kept secret. George, Thomas, Bertram, Mitch and Charlie stood again in a circle trying to work out a plan of action. Although Charlie was not going to be part of the team, he was just there to witness the exciting plans the team might come up with. It wasn't because Charlie was afraid, he just wouldn't be quick enough and he had been wounded in the last skirmish and nobody wanted to risk him getting hurt again.

Among Brian's toys there was a remote controlled helicopter. Thomas remembered seeing it advertised on television and Brian saying, 'Can I have one for Christmas?' That was a couple of years ago. Brian had played with it once and lost control and the helicopter came down and the rotor came off, so he never bothered with it again.

George said, 'If it is broken, it won't be any good to us.'

'We might be able to repair it,' said Thomas 'I'll see if I can find it in Brian's toy cupboard.'

Thomas's sleek body moved effortlessly up the stairs to the spare bedroom, which was where all the unwanted junk was kept. Although it was unwanted, they kept it in case it turned out to be useful in the future. Thomas pushed the door open. None of the doors were ever shut upstairs because Brian, when fit and healthy, usually crashed through doors at great speed when playing one of his favourite games "Dick Barton Special Agent."

Thomas found the helicopter and all the bits and pieces, the remote, spare batteries and a bag of odds and ends. He laid the bag on its side and nosed everything in. He picked up the bag in his teeth and half dragged it down the stairs. With each step it thumped and he was expecting any minute his human mother and father to appear, but they didn't and eventually he reached the kitchen and went through the cat flap and out in the garden and dumped everything by the fence. He went to the hole in the fence and dug out some more earth. He picked up the bag and pulled it backwards through the gap. By the time he got the bag to where all the others were he was slightly out of breath and he sat down.

Chapter 15

Thomas said between gulps of breath that he had seen a Sherman Tank and a few other mechanical toys which may be useful in their plan of action, but how that was yet to be decided. Luckily for the gang, Nick had built his nest at the bottom of Thomas's garden. None of them wanted to go into the woods as it was too dark and foreboding. Bertram said 'I really can't see how we are going to use the helicopter, unless we get Brian interested in flying it.'

Thomas said 'How are we going to do that?'

Bertram said 'Leave the helicopter down here in the middle of the garden and hopefully he will see it from his bedroom window and get enthusiastic about it again.'

'You hope,' said Thomas.

Bertram said, 'That's the only chance we have that I can think of apart from climbing the tree. It's a long way up.'

Thomas looked at the tree and guessed it could possibly be forty feet high and thought to himself, 'if I could climb it at night and wait until daylight then Nick would have to leave the nest to get food, but his wife would be there guarding their baby – perhaps not a good idea.'

Bertram said 'We'll need a diversion and if someone could operate the helicopter, if and when it gets repaired, Thomas could climb the tree and we might succeed in getting the ring back.

Help came from an unexpected quarter. The human father came into the garden in his working clothes to do some gardening and he saw the helicopter in pieces on the lawn. He said, 'I wonder how this got out here?' He picked up the helicopter and rotor and the other bits and pieces and walked off towards the shed.

Two hours later he emerged with the toy which appeared to be completely repaired and went into the house. Thomas followed to see where he was going and whether that piece of equipment was going to be on hand for their use later on. He noted the human father plug a lead into the helicopter and the other end into a socket on the wall and switched it on. He then placed four large batteries into the remote and extended a rod and switched it on and Thomas noticed a light had come on. The human father turned off the remote and laid it down on the table. He then went outside to his shed, picked up his garden fork and spade and headed for his vegetable garden.

Thomas sauntered out of the house and told George what he had seen. It looks like we will be able to use the flying machine tonight. Thomas said, 'It will be ideal as this one has lights on it and you can switch them on and off from the remote.'

'How do you know all this?' said George.

'Television!' said Thomas. 'Brian saw this helicopter being advertised and asked his parents if he could have one for Christmas.'

George said, 'It's a good job you like watching television.'

Thomas said 'Yes! Isn't it. We do have another problem though, the helicopter is plugged into the wall being charged up and tonight might not be ideal to go into action, as neither of us will be capable of unplugging the machine from the wall.'

'Hmm!' said George. 'What about Bertram, he might be able to do that.' 'No!' said Thomas 'His pudgy paws, won't let him do that.

' George said 'We seem to be up a gum tree then.'

'We'll have to sleep on it tonight.' said Thomas.

George and Thomas decided after they had eaten their tea to sleep together just in case an opportunity arose that night.

Chapter 16

Dawn was at six am the next day, a fine day, not much of a breeze. Thomas said, 'Looks like a good day to go flying. But first I must do the most important thing first.'

'What's that?' said George.

'Eat!' said Thomas 'and I'll meet you back at the kennel later.'

Both went to their respective kitchens.

Brian was allowed up today as his father said he had repaired his helicopter and was going to give it a trial run. Brian didn't want to leave his bedroom because he would see the flight far better from his window.

Bertram and Mitch were beginning to get a funny tingling sensation and couldn't understand what was happening to them. Mitch whose eyes stared with a glassy look was able to see and Bertram's eyelids fluttered and then opened.

Brian was leaning out of the window, looking at his father trying to get the helicopter to fly. Both Bertram and Mitch were wondering if this was a dream and Bertram pinched himself and said, 'ouch,' in a loud voice. Brian turned round and seeing nothing out of place continued to look out of the window.

'Oh dear!' whispered Bertram 'My dream is coming true. I dreamt this might happen and it did happen In my dream.

'When was this?' Mitch whispered back.

'A couple of days ago.' said Bertram.

Brian turned round and said 'Will you two stop chattering and come and watch my father trying to fly this helicopter.'

Bertram and Mitch nearly fell off the shelf in amazement. Brian could hear them talking and he must know they can walk as well. They jumped off the shelf and joined Brian at the window. Looking at the garden so early in the morning gave the toys a different view and then this thing rose in the air and it looked as if was firing something and the toys and Brian ducked. The human father shouted out that it was a light that came on and off quickly, better to see at night. The thing flew round the garden three times before landing five feet away from Thomas.

Thomas didn't get up as he wanted to show everybody he really wasn't interested in such childish behaviour and of course, he was not aware of the drama that was happening in Brian's bedroom. Bertram was believing it was a dream and kept on pinching himself but it always hurt him so obviously he was not asleep. It had to be true.

Bertram said to Brian 'This will have to be our secret, you can't and you mustn't tell anyone else that you have two bears that can talk and walk.' Brian said, 'How long have you had these powers?'

'Not long.' said Bertram 'We used to only come alive when you went to sleep, you're not asleep, are you?'

Brian said 'I don't think so Bertram! I'll pinch myself just make sure.' Brian did that and said 'Ouch!' very loudly. 'No! I am not.'

A promised pact was achieved and like the three musketeers they pledged their secret.

Bertram said 'Ahh! We do have another secret you need to keep Brian.' 'What's that?' said Brian.

'Thomas, your cat and George the dog next door!'

'What about them?' said Brian.

Bertram was not sure whether Brian would be able to take on board another surprise, so he said 'It will have to be the five musketeers.' Brian was slightly taken aback and said 'You're kidding me.'

'No! We're not.' said Bertram.

Brian got dressed quickly unable to control his eagerness to meet Thomas and George on different terms and he knew he must keep their secret safe. What a pity though, the only boy who could really talk to animals and toy bears in plain English.

Chapter 17

Brian eventually came down and met the gang of four very briefly before going off to have his breakfast.

George had managed to squeeze himself under the fence. He wasn't a very large dog, about the same length as Bertram, just a big bark. When Brian appeared again, he wanted to know what plans they had for the day.

Bertram brought Brian up to speed relating the story of how Nick the Magpie had stolen his mother's ring when she was washing up one evening and had flown up in the tree at the bottom of the garden.

Brian thought what a naughty magpie and said to Bertram

'I suppose he can speak as well.'

'Yes!' said Bertram.

Brian said 'Why can't we ask him to return the ring.'

'Well for one thing he would lose his credibility with the bird kingdom and another thing, magpies always feel that the more items they have in the nest when their children are born, they will grow big and strong and able to leave the nest earlier to start their own family.'

Thomas said suddenly, 'Curtain rings!'

'Curtain rings?' said Bertram 'What about them?'

Thomas said 'We could get lots of curtain rings, polish them up and replace them for the ring, that should do the trick.'

Bertram seemed impressed with the idea and asked Brian if his mother had spare curtain rings in the house. Brian said he would ask.

Bertram said, 'What are you going to say if she asks you why you want them?'

'I'll cross that bridge if and when I come to it.' said Brian.

He thought he would take the bull by the horns and ask that all important question. 'Mum have we any spare curtain rings?'

'Yes!' she answered. 'What do you want them for?'

'I was thinking of using them in my Meccano Set, I have a project in mind and I'm lacking some bits and pieces,' said Brian.

'I have twenty large brass curtain rings that are out of fashion, you can have those, if they will help with your project.'

'They will do very nicely.' said Brian. 'Thank you mum!'

Brian reported back to the gang and they thought he had done a good job. They were very cloudy in colour and

Thomas said 'We need to polish them up so they are nice and shiny.'

So he asked Brian if he could get some Brasso. That was going to be a bit more tricky to ask about. Brian thought long and hard. If asked why he wanted to polish them up, it was obvious he couldn't tell her. So he asked his mother.

His mother said okay without asking for a reason as it seemed clear to her that brass curtain rings would need to glitter if they were to show up in Brian's project. She gave Brian a tin of Brasso and a duster and instructed him how to use it.

Brian reported back to the gang and again the gang said how well he had done.

'What's next?' said Brian.

'We clean and polish the curtain rings until they sparkle,' said Bertram. 'and then we'll have to wait till dusk before making our next move.' Brian said 'My parents say I must go to bed early until my health improves a bit more.'

'You will need to get up and sneak on down, because you are vital to our plans tonight,' said Bertram

'What do you want me to do?'

'You have to fly the helicopter.' said George.

Brian looked at each face of the gang in a slow motion. 'I can't do that.' said Brian.

'Nor can we!' said Mitch holding up his pudgy paws.

Thomas said 'You'll have to think like a Commando and do your best. You are my diversion because I will be climbing the tree with six brass curtain rings in my mouth in exchange for your mother's ring.

George will be doing worrying tactics at the foot of the tree and Mitch and Bertram have set up a pulley system to gain access to the first branch, so it looks like a frontal assault. We need you to fly the helicopter as close to the nest as possible, putting the light on in short blasts. Don't let us down Brian.'

Chapter 18

Seven o'clock arrived and Brian protested as he always did about going to bed so as not to arouse suspicion. The human father always read him a short story before he went off to sleep. Only this time Brian just had to keep awake. He woke up at nine pm. Was he too late. He looked out of his window. No one was there, but then he remembered they would all be by the tree.

Bertram and Mitch were on the first branch wondering whether Brian was going to play his part. Bertram wondered whether they could lasso the next branch and he was tossing up the spare rope trying to get it over the branch, but not having much luck. Thomas was two feet away from the branch where Nick's nest was and had lost two curtain rings when his tail got snagged on a forked thick twig. He opened his mouth briefly to say ouch and the rings dropped from his mouth. George was running round the tree silently. Then all of a sudden they heard a noise like a whirlwind as the blades sliced through the air and lights from the helicopter seemed to flash in short intervals. The noise got nearer. The precision flying by Brian was outstanding.

Nick was beside himself and he was the only one in the nest which dazzled with different gems. He flew away and Thomas leapt forward and dropped the brass curtain rings into the nest and collected five assorted pieces of jewellery.

One of the rings he dropped and watched it as it fell hitting one branch then another until it reached Bertram who did a leap like a goalie and managed to catch the ring in his paw. Luckily he fell into a bush. Thomas found that coming down was easier than it had been to climb, which is unusual for a cat.

Brian was no where to be seen and yet the helicopter was still flying round the nest. Thomas reached the bottom of the tree and saw with amazement that it was the human father. Thomas was going to make himself scarce. Bertram stayed in the bush. Mitch stood as close to the tree trunk as possible and George ran round the other side of tree when Brian's father appeared on the scene. They couldn't be seen. 'I can't get the helicopter to come down.'

No one spoke. 'I know you're all here!'

Slowly but surely Bertram came out of the bush, Thomas and George appeared and Mitch climbed down the tree.

Brian's father said 'The helicopter won't come down! The helicopter won't come down!'

Brian woke up. His mother and father were in his room with worried looks on their faces. Mother said, 'You've been very ill and delirious, but the doctor said once the fever broke you would be okay.'

Chapter 19

His mother and father left the room to allow Brian to rest and Brian closed his eyes momentarily and then thought about Bertram and Mitch. He sat up quickly and looked round the room. Bertram was on the window sill with Mitch on the shelf. They were quite still. Brian leaned forward and picked up Bertram. He felt the warmth of the fur and thought Bertram was really alive, but it was the morning sun's rays that had been shining on him.

He looked across at Mitch on the shelf and saw the stony, glassy stare. 'Only toys!' said Brian to himself.

He got out of bed and went to the window and saw Thomas curled up in his usual place soaking up the sun and looked next door and George the dog was half in and half out of his kennel chewing a bone. It was all a dream said Brian to himself. It seemed so real.

His Mother came into the room and told Brian to get back into his bed, he was to stay there for a day or two and she told him that she had lost her wedding ring, but found it by the old tree down the garden.

She said she probably lost it hanging out some washing a couple of days before, also she had found his old helicopter. It was hanging from the same tree two branches below a Magpie's nest. 'They have two baby magpies. It's so nice to have birds in the garden again.

Thomas has made friends with George the dog next door and often sleeps with him.'

'What would you like for breakfast?' His mother asked as she went out of his room. 'My usual please.' said Brian. His mother brought his porridge and a glass of orange juice.

Brian put Bertram back on the shelf and stared at him. Did his eyes deceive him but did Bertram wink back at him?

The end

About Amanda Breach

Amanda Breach is an Illustrator based in Eastbourne, East Sussex.

She achieved a BA Honours degree in Illustration at Middlesex university in London and now works as a freelance illustrator.

Amanda works in a variety of media for her work including traditional watercolour painting, pencil work and digital art. She has worked on a variety of Projects ranging from children's illustrated books to stationary, shop fonts and advertising.

Amanda enjoys working from her home and garden where she has created a unique range of Little Fox greeting cards. In Amanda's spare time she loves to take her sketchbook around with her and draw at different locations.

You can find out more about Amanda and see more of her work on her website www.amandabreachillustrations.com

Mithra Publishing Company

Printed in Great Britain
by Amazon